J
PICTURE   London, Jonathan,
           1947-

           Sun dance, water
           dance.

$15.99

DATE			

SUN DANCE
WATER DANCE

SUN DANCE

Dutton Children's Books
NEW YORK

WATER DANCE

BY Jonathan London

ILLUSTRATED BY Greg Couch

CIP Data is available.

Published in the United States 2001 by Dutton Children's Books,

a division of Penguin Putnam Books for Young Readers

345 Hudson Street, New York, New York 10014

www.penguinputnam.com

ISBN 0-525-46682-7

Designed by Alan Carr

Printed in Hong Kong • First Edition

10 9 8 7 6 5 4 3 2 1

For Bob, Pat, David & Leah, Maureen, Aaron, Sean & Ryan—
with thanks to Karen   J.L.

To Peter de S., Robin, and Emily. Thanks for making this one
of the best, most carefree summers ever.   G.C.

We play in the sun
like a dance

dally in the brilliance
of heat
      radiating
off our shining bodies

till the sweat
              pours
from our pores and we laugh
at the heat
like a sun burning
inside us
till we can't
take it anymore

and dash down
the narrow path
to the fast green river

to plunge the heat
away
          feel
the chill ripple
down our spines
                    feel
that snowmelt water
from the high mountains
in our blood
our bones turn
to icicles
and we giggle
with the tickle
of our skin tightened
into goose bumps
and splash and wiggle

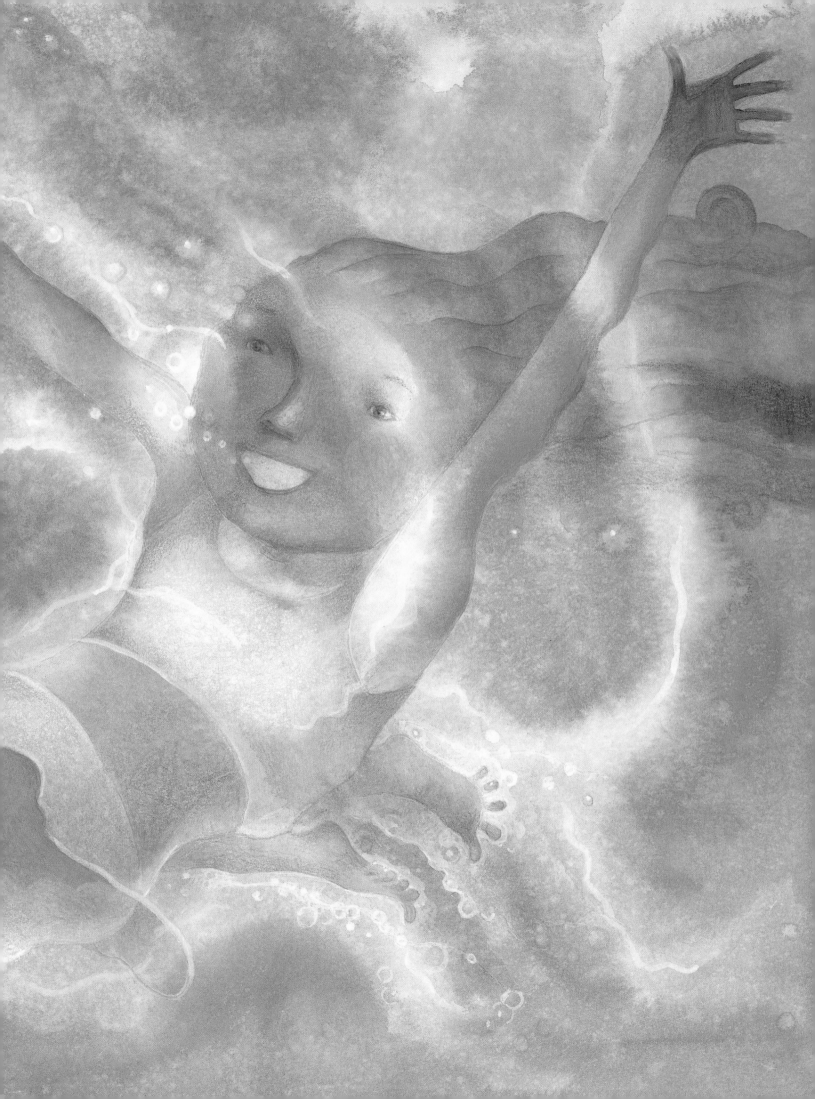

then climb out
to skip flat stones
across a glass pool
aim and fire
round stones at a rock
target
      and watch it topple
with a perfect
blow
      "Yes!"

hop
on an old inner tube
    bob down the bubbly current

    kick and hand-paddle
to the side and out

walk back barefoot tenderly
over smooth
sun-warmed river stones
and toss the tube
in again

hop on
       and away
ride that little rapid
in a wide arc
out and around

and back to shore
careful for snakes

and the sharp bite
of rocks
like arrowheads

picnic on chips and fruit
laugh in the sunlight
under trees shaking leaves
in the bright wind
the willows with their feet
in the water
the alder angling out of sheer
rock
and higher up
pine and fir against the sky
                    dragging the eye

up
and into blue and too-bright
sun

race
back to the cabin
up the winding
rocky path
in through wood door
grab a drink from the cooler
crack it open
ice cold down gullet

Ahhhhhh!

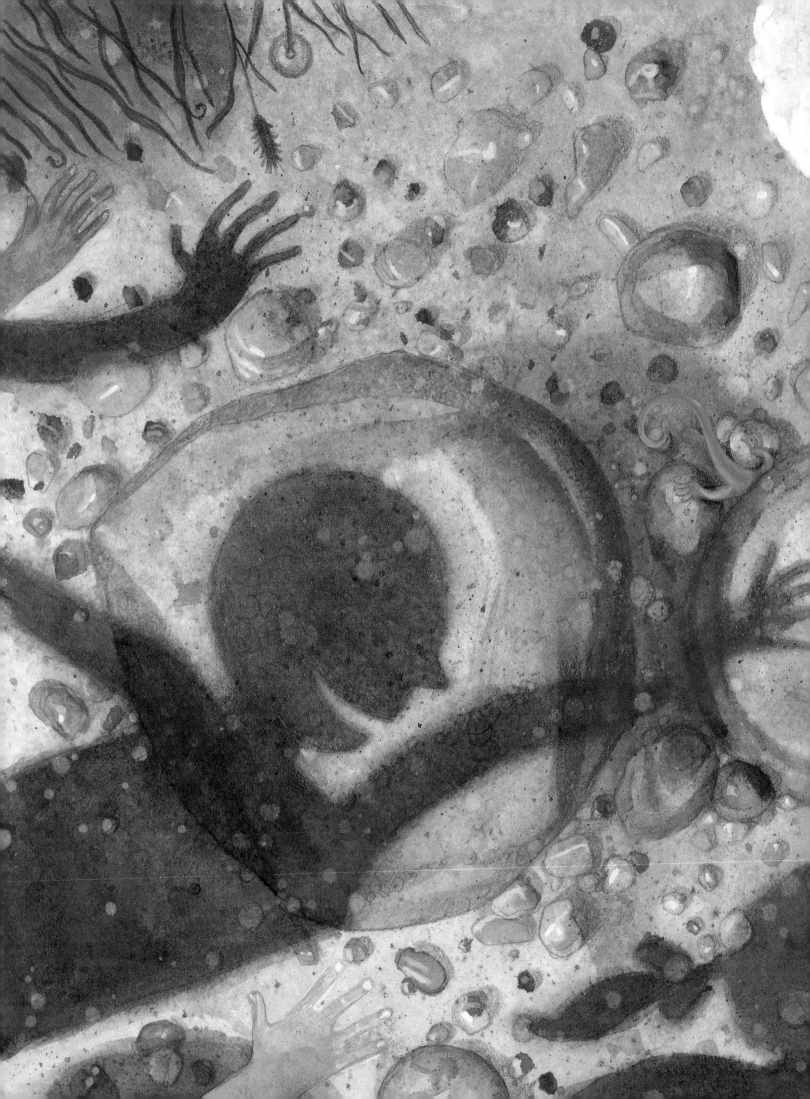

and back out
into the hot sun
to chase lizards
under boulders

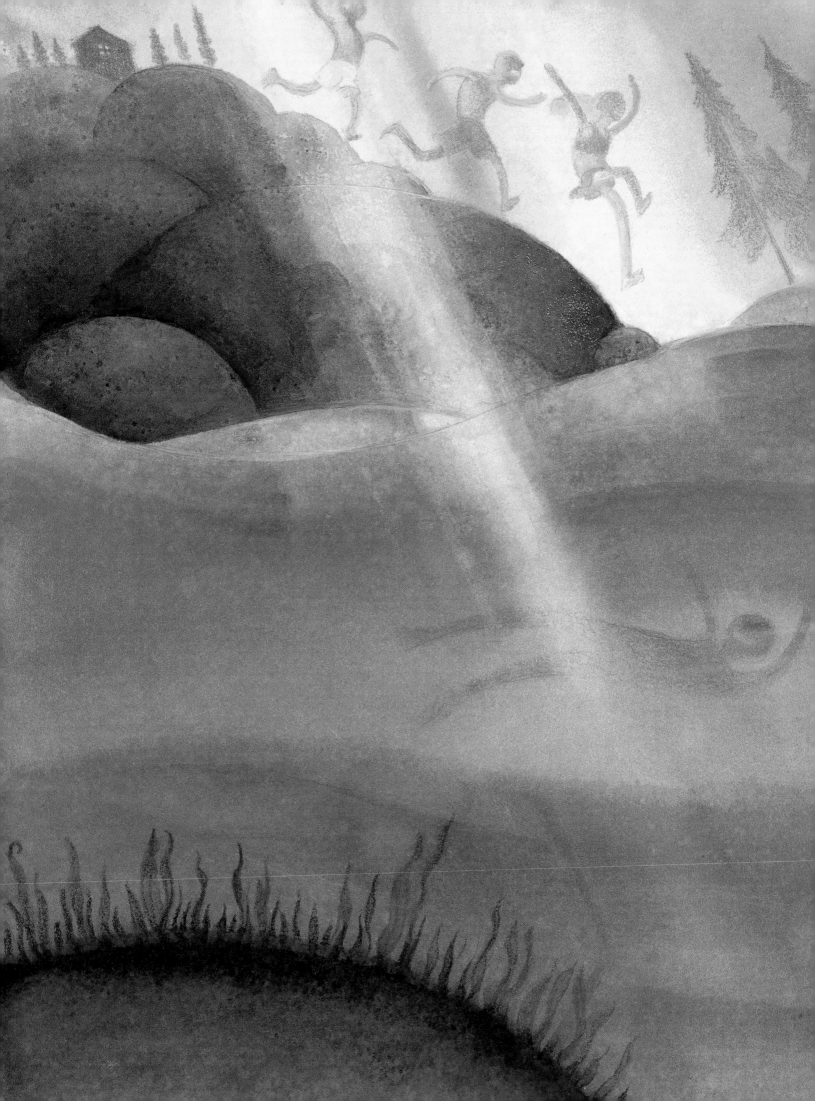

till the sweat pours
again
and again foot-slap down to the
cold river
diving into green worlds
of icy light
twist and roll like a river otter
soaking in the full
life of the whole Earth

when the light
fades
and the first star
comes out
make a wish
and hug a boulder

                           holding

the last heat

lie in the grass
and watch the moon float
like a great boat
and Orion march across the sky
and the stars

shoot

"There's one!"
"There's one!"

till the air
chills

then back to the cabin
to dream of hot sun
cold water
bright days

and flickering nights